The Octo...
The Thun...

Other Books by Carrie Duggan:
The Author's Library

To all my friends, wherever you may be.
I'm forever grateful for you all.

This is not a love story.

I

Saturday, August 31st, 2019

At first glance, April Bloom lived the perfect life: Fawn's Hill was a dreamy place to live; she was happily married and her bakery business was thriving. But it had also been at least six months since her husband had promised her a date night and April couldn't remember the last time they spent time together, just the two of them. Despite working hard at *Sweet Cakes Bakery*, it finished every weekday at 5pm but this wasn't the case for her husband. He seemed to spend more time in the office than he ever did at home, especially over the last year.

They were going to go out for dinner but when it was forecast to be the worst storm that the village has had in years, they decided to stay in. They'd bought a couple of pizzas, bottles of wine and planned to watch something on *Netflix*. April had been looking forward to this all week and spent hours cleaning the house until it was perfect. She wore a dress that flattered her figure and heels that made her taller; as well as covering the freckles on her face with powder and smoky eyeshadow to make her green eyes twinkle. Then, she finally straightened her wild, ginger hair until perfectly framed her face

But just as the pizzas went into the oven and the timer was set, April's husband had gotten a call and had to get back to the office, again. Immediately.

'I'm so sorry, baby.' He muttered, as he grabbed his briefcase, which hadn't been unpacked, yet.

April could see the glimpse of disappointment in his eyes. 'Do you know when you'll be back?'

'I reckon it'll be all night,' he replied, as he grabbed his coat and umbrella. 'They need to call an emergency meeting and if I'm not there, the client's gonna pull out of the deal.'

'Can't Martin cover for you?'

'Apparently he's made plans with his

missus. Again.'

'So did we.'

April's husband gave her a quick peck on the lips. It was so swift that she almost didn't feel it.

'I promise I'll make it up to you.'

'Sure.'

'I mean it this time.'

'I know.'

'I'll keep you updated. I love you,' he said, just before he headed out the door.

'Love you too.'

A few seconds later the oven timer went off but April had suddenly lost her appetite and instead she quickly drank two large glasses of wine, which went straight to her head. She slumped onto her sofa and stared up at the ceiling, her heart heavy with frustration. It felt like her living room was spinning rapidly, while also getting bigger. A part of her wished she had kicked up a fuss and demanded him to stay, because she was sick of falling for his unfulfilled promises. But she never did, because she didn't want to be a bother and therefore kept her disappointment internal. The silence screaming through the house was all too familiar these days.

Sometimes, April forgot what her husband did for a living. Bloody Martin, he always had a stupid excuse and got away with it all the time. April remembered the last dinner party, where she realised that he was an arrogant berk and the size of his briefcase was definitely compensating for something. Whilst his wife boasted in every other sentence that she went to Oxford University and apparently she's the one-hundred-and-thirty-seventh person in line for the throne. Of course, April never told her husband, but she wished that there were someone she could joke about it with.

She sighed, heavily. April and her husband had always supported each other, when it came to their careers. Before she opened *Sweet Cakes Bakery*, April was growing her small business, whilst still living at her grandparents.

Her husband said that he loved seeing her passion shine through with every cake she baked; even though he'd never seen her crying on the kitchen floor because she couldn't make her crumb-coat even. There were days when April wanted to scream and throw her oven gloves out of the window after baking and decorating two-hundred gluten-free cupcakes for a last-minute wedding.

But even though April was also super proud of what her husband had achieved, she couldn't help but think that his career was like a third person in their marriage and it demanded most of his time. He woke up two hours before she did, worked longer hours than anyone else in the office and always came home exhausted. But despite all this, she just wished that he could put some time into her, too.

They had moved to Fawn's Hill just over three years ago and lived on the edge of the village. From the outside it was picturesque: located at the bottom of a hill, with cobbled streets and beautiful families living in identical cottages. It was certainly a change from the town April used to live in: where she'd fall asleep to the hustle and bustle of car alarms and police sirens, blaring down the street; as well as hearing all the drunk people singing loudly on a Monday night. But for April, all the noise and the rabble felt like home. Whereas in Fawn's Hill, everyone was so polite to each other during the day and then the nights were eerily quiet. It was a place where every generation had grown up together, all living their perfect lives and they would get together to talk about how wonderful everything was. It seemed like everyone in Fawn's Hill was able to balance everything: be happy all the time, while maintaining an active social life. But even though everyone seemed friendly enough, they would also roll their eyes and tut if you did something weird. It was an expression that April was all too familiar with, although she was desperate to be accepted.

There was one occasion where April went to a barbeque and no-one ate the cheesecake she made because of the one vegan who kicked up a fuss. Another time, someone was running seventy-five miles for their favourite charity (Babies in Britain Born with Chubby Ankles) and everyone thought April was stingy for donating twenty pounds when they all gave over a hundred. Even though she spent a lot of her time helping out at bake sales and summer fairs, it was never enough. She tried to make new friends but felt like an imposter; it seemed like nobody in Fawn's Hill wanted her around, but they were too polite to say anything. There wasn't anyone in the village that she could call a friend; no one that she could completely relax with.

So over the years, April slowly grew a desire for perfection. She never left the house without looking her best and pretended that everything was wonderful, all the time. She tried to act like everyone else, just so she could fit in. Her cottage was so tidy, it was almost too pristine to call home. Gradually, she became obsessed in order to meet the high expectations of everyone else. Just the thought of showing any vulnerability struck anxiety into her heart because she didn't want anyone to be aware of how lonely she felt. She didn't even want to admit it to herself.

April slowly got up off the sofa and sat on her windowsill, to watch the thunderstorm. She used to do this all the time when she lived with her grandparents; it always soothed her and she could focus on what was happening outside, rather than what was going on inside her head. Everyone was tucked away indoors, so there was no pressure to go out and socialise. The rain was slowly getting heavier, smacking against the windows with a dull thud. The wind rattled through the trees, making the leaves dance on their branches, with thunder and lightning working in tandem to make themselves known. A part of April wanted to go jumping in puddles, but she dismissed the idea instantly because she knew it wasn't sensible. Besides, what would the neighbours think? So instead, she watched two droplets of rain come together and trickle down her window, before splitting off and landing at the bottom.

She then reached in her pocket and took out the small, crochet octopus that she always carried around with her. She called him Watson, after her grandpa because he was the one who made it for her when she was little. He was made from a soft, purple wool with beady eyes and was small enough to fit in the palm of her hand. He lived in her pocket, as April tried to navigate her way through life and became especially useful when she moved to Fawn's Hill; he poked out of her apron, as she baked from Monday to Friday and he sat on her bedside table, looking over April as she slept. There weren't many people who knew about Watson the Octopus.

Whenever she was nervous, April would hold onto him, for a sense of security, a reminder that everything was going to be okay. This was something she did as she cried herself to sleep every night, whilst she was growing up at her parent's house. When April moved in with her grandparent's at sixteen, she'd finally found a place that she could call home.

As boredom crept across her entire body, April began doom-scrolling through her phone. Her most recent posts on Instagram were meticulously perfect, taken at the right angles with the most flattering filters. It was a way to consistently prove to everyone that she was living her best life. There was one photo that April and her husband took at that dinner party, with gleaming smiles on their faces; but April remembered crying in the bathroom just twenty minutes beforehand, because Martin had said that she was as dumb as a rock. But she would never share that, online.

Yet the further she scrolled back through all her photos, April began to notice small imperfections in each one. She used to smile with her crooked teeth on show and that was something she would never do, nowadays. There was one photo of her in mid-laughter, showing her double-chin; there's another where she was sat in the local chippy after the club, with a drunk smile on her face and ketchup on her chin. But April noticed how genuinely happy she was because she was too busy enjoying life, rather than striving for perfection all the time. In her early twenties, April was fearless and never cared about what other people thought of her. She may have danced like a fool and sang out of tune, but she was allowing herself to have fun.

Facebook reminded her of a festival that she went to, twelve years ago. April stared at a photo captioned: *BEST. WEEKEND. EVER!* She's covered in glitter and sitting on Noah's shoulders, her pale thighs dangling down his chest.

April doesn't even think she shaved her legs and her hair definitely needed a wash, at the time. But she smiled at the memory. It was Noah who took April to her first festival and she soaked up every minute of it. The music blasted from every stage and the sun was beaming down on them, as they linked arms and stumbled through the crowds, gradually getting sweatier and covered in dust. They clung onto each other, as they threw themselves into the mosh pit, both screaming with laughter. But when they went to go and see one of their favourite acts, they were at the back of the crowd and whilst Noah was tall enough to see over people's heads, April had to jump around like a lunatic just to catch a glimpse of the stage.

'Do you want to sit on my shoulders?' he asked her, trying not to laugh.

'No, thanks,' April replied, stubbornly. 'I'll be fine.'

'Suit yourself.'

During the next two songs, April was constantly out of breath from dodging around people and jumping to see over their heads. She was so preoccupied with trying to see the stage that she couldn't enjoy the music.

'Wow, this performance is amazing!' Noah said, loudly, looking back at April. 'If only you could see it though…'

'Oh, shush.'

'My offer still stands?'

April looked up Noah and even though she didn't want to give in, she reluctantly nodded. Instantly, Noah grabbed her by the hand and swooped her onto his shoulders. Their singing was drowned out by the screaming crowds and iconic guitar solos. But April remembered throwing her hands in the air and smiling so hard that her cheeks ached. It was a special moment shared between best friends. Nothing else mattered. April would do anything to go back to feeling that way.

Noah Wisdom. They used to be inseparable, as close as brother and sister. There were times where they'd be out until 4am or they would watch bad movies at home and eat too much takeout. They even spent an entire summer travelling around Europe, just the two of them. They found cheap tickets and just went wherever they wanted, with no plan in mind. But they were never lost because Noah always knew exactly where to go and met the best people along the way. They stayed up to watch the sunrise over the Berlin Gate and had everyone sing Bowie in an underground bar in the Ukraine. It was one of the best summers of her life.

Noah was a friend to everyone but never wanted to settle down in one place. He jumped around from job to job; from night shifts at the pub to days spent working in retail. He politely declined anyone who fancied him and continued to travel to every extraordinary corner of the world, even after April moved to Fawn's Hill. Eventually, their lives went in very different directions.

But Noah was the only one who truly understood April and he was also the only friend who knew about Watson the Octopus. April wondered what he was up to, right now. It had been three years since they last spoke, so he could be doing anything, anywhere in the world. She still had his number in her phone, but did she have the confidence to call him? Before she could talk herself out of it, she hit the call button and pressed the phone tight against her ear. He picked up on the first ring.

'April Bloom,' He said, almost sounding speechless.

'Hey, Noah,' April muttered, nervously.

'How've you been, sis?'

'I'm...' Just the sound of his voice brought April's heartbeat down to a reasonable rate. Whenever Noah was with her, anywhere felt like a safe space; where April could say anything to him, without judgement. But as much as she wanted to say everything on her mind, she suddenly drew back.

'I'm fine,' she slurred.

'Really? You don't sound it. Have you

been drinking wine?'

'Only two glasses...'

'It's good to know you still can't hold your drink,' he teased her.

'Shush.'

'So, what's up?'

'I... I just wanted to hear your voice, again,' she admitted, her cheeks flushing. 'I'm home alone...'

'Where's your fella?'

'He's working. Again.'

'Ah, that sucks.'

'Bloody Martin. I blame him for this!'

'Who's Martin?'

'He's a twat.'

'Ouch.'

The two of them laughed and it felt like nothing had changed, between them. It reminded April of when they used to hang out at her grandparents'; sitting opposite each other on the sofa for hours, chatting and laughing away. It felt comfortable, just like old times.

'April?'

'Yeah?'

'It's good to hear from you, too.'

'Maybe you could come over tonight?' April asked, not thinking twice. Suddenly, her heart sank to the bottom of her stomach and she was filled with embarrassment, thinking about how desperate she sounded.

'April, I-'

'You're busy, I get that,' she said quickly, before Noah could finish. 'I bet you're trekking across volcanoes or saving a clan of baby orangutans. It's been so long, what was I thinking...'

'Funnily enough, I'm trekking across a volcano to save the baby orangutans next week,' he joked, before April could spiral any further. 'I'm free tonight.'

'You don't have to, if you don't wanna. Also, there's the thunderstorm…'

'Of course I want to! You know I'll always make time for my bestie. Besides, someone has to hold your hair back, whilst you throw up.'

'I'm not that drunk!'

'You're not fooling me! So I'll see you in about an hour?'

'See you then, bro.'

When April put the phone down, a smile grew across her face. She continued to watch the thunderstorm, waiting patiently for Noah to arrive. All whilst thinking back on old times.

II

Friday, March 10th, 2006

'You alright, mate? Can I get you anything?'

'Two double G&T's, four lagers and twelve shots of vodka. How much?!'

'Can someone change the barrel for the cider? I've got to pour five of these.'

Beer sloshed over glasses and the roar of drunken punters was fairly standard for a Friday night at The Two Arrows. April dreaded these shifts because by the end of the working week, people were exhausted and wanted to forget everything by the time they reached the end of the glass. The floor was suspiciously sticky and stuck to the soles of your trainers. The entire pub was filled to capacity, the bar five-people deep. Live music from the local Irish band was deafening but none of this was new to eighteen-year-old April. She'd been working in the pub for about six months now. Long enough for her to be pulling twelve hour shifts but not enough time to joke about the manager being a miserable twat.

  Her colleagues were friendly enough but she didn't know them that well. There was talk of some new bouncer who apparently was an absolute legend. But to be honest, April had become quite lonely since all her friends had gone to university and she went straight into work. Right now, she was too preoccupied with dodging drunken customers and stacking up empty glasses. The bar wasn't going to close for another two hours and she could feel herself becoming delirious. She'd already smashed several glasses and despite the freezing thunderstorm, it was boiling inside from the amount of body heat that was shared between strangers.

When shifts at The Two Arrows became too stressful (as they usually did at the weekends), April would hold onto Watson the Octopus and find a sense of relief. But she let out a small shriek and dropped another two glasses when she realised that her pockets were empty. April's heart began to pound beneath her t-shirt. Pouring pints for punters didn't mean anything to her, anymore. Dropping to her knees she crawled across the pub floor and began to search for Watson. She retraced her steps and looked down in the cellar that stank of stale lager and piss, the stockroom and the staff toilets. The stench of sweat made April's stomach churn, but she persisted. Maybe she dropped it outside, when she said hello to the bouncer and offered him a cookie? That was just before he'd had to break up that bar fight. But just before her manager could find her, April rushed to the entrance.

Nope. Watson wasn't outside, either.

There was still an hour to go before the bar closed but April couldn't think of anything else. She sunk to the floor, hugged her knees to her chest and stared into the distance. The thunder was rumbling and the rain was dripping down her face, smudging her thick, black eyeliner. April had never lost Watson before; it was like losing a part of herself. Without him in her pocket, she suddenly felt very unsafe. She began to think about how much it would upset her grandpa, because she promised him that she'd always keep Watson safe. Then April remembered the constant disappointment, from her parents. They always said that she would never be as good as her brothers and despised the fact that she didn't go to University and ended up working in a pub. Maybe her parents would've been proud of her, if she had just done what they wanted? Had she made a mistake, over the last six months? She was always going to be a disappointment…

'Are you okay?'

April looked up and saw the bouncer sat next to her. He towered over her like a gentle giant and his kind smile slowly put April's mind at ease. He had dark skin, broad shoulders, thick arms, as well as several piercings in his ears and large hands with stubby, bitten nails. A Guns N' Roses t-shirt poked through his thick fleece and practical raincoat, accompanied by a bobble hat crammed over his curls. The look in his eyes were warm and comforting, like a hug from an old friend.

'No. Life is terrible,' April replied and stared back down at her trainers.

'Don't say that. Life can be amazing if you-'

'I've lost Watson!'

'Who's Watson?'

'He's an octopus.'

'Watson the Octopus?'

'I've looked everywhere but I can't find him.'

'Have you checked the local aquarium?'

'If you're not going to say anything

helpful, you can sod off…'

'Wait a minute, is this what you're talking about?'

He reached into his pocket and April gasped in delight, as a small, crochet octopus sat in the palm of his hand.

'That's him!' April threw her arms around the friendly bouncer and hugged him tight. 'You have no idea how much this means to me.'

'I can tell.' He said, reassuringly, as the two broke apart.

'Where did you find him?'

'You must have dropped him, when you were caught in that bar fight. I found him on the floor, so I thought I'd keep him safe.'

'Well, thanks,' April muttered. 'Maybe life isn't that terrible.'

'I told you so.' He clambered onto his feet and helped April up. 'I'm Noah, by the way.'

'Hiya. I'm-'

'April! Where the bloody hell have you been?'

Her heart dropped. April completely

forgot that she was still on shift and as she slowly turned around, her manager, Jamie, was storming through the crowds with a furious look on his face. He looked like a scarecrow, but he also put the fear of God into her.

'I'm really sorry…' she muttered, as she tried to avoid her manager's gaze.

'You've been gone for almost an hour. What have you been playing at?'

'Err…'

'It's not her fault,' Noah replied, quickly. 'She got caught in the middle of a bar fight and I've been looking after her. Happy staff, happy pub, after all.'

April looked at Noah and mouthed a word of thanks. Then, she looked back at Jamie, who'd become speechless. Nobody ever spoke back to him.

'I hope you're alright, April,' Jamie muttered, just before he shuffled away. 'You can stay behind the bar, until we close.'

'I really owe you for that,' April said to Noah.

'Don't worry about it,' Noah replied,

casually. He handed April the octopus. 'So, this is yours?'

April took Watson and shoved him in her pocket, giving him a reassuring squeeze. 'Thanks again.'

'Hey, April,' Noah called out, just before she disappeared back into the pub. 'Cool t-shirt, by the way.'

April looked down and realised that it was the same as Noah's. She smiled back at him.

'Thanks. You too.'

*

Since their first meeting, April's life in The Two Arrows soon became a lot easier. Even when she arrived for her shift the next evening, Noah greeted her with a high-five and a bear hug and it felt as if they had been friends for years. As the weeks slowly progressed, they quickly felt comfortable around each other. Whenever the crowds were calm, April would join Noah at the front of the pub for a few minutes and bring him pints of coke to keep him awake. When

Noah brought empty glasses to the bar, he kept an eye out for any creepy customers that gawked from afar.

'Creepy-Alan's staring at you, again,' Noah muttered to April, as she poured two pints of stout.

'For God's sake, why?' April whined. 'It's bad enough those two are at it tonight.'

The two of them looked to their right at the drunken couple who were sloppily making out at the side of the bar.

'How long have they been at it?' Noah asked, as he tried to hold back his laughter.

'For about half an hour,'

'Blimey! David Attenborough could make an hour-long documentary on them. It like a weird, mating dance. And so sloppy, too! Don't they know how to breathe?'

'Creepy-Alan's still staring at me…'

'Look, if he tries anything, then let me know. I've got your back.'

April smiled and quickly poured him

a coke. 'Thanks, Noah.'

That night, Creepy-Alan tried to drag April onto his lap but just before she could smack him, Noah immediately swooped in threw him out. Then, he wrapped his arms around April and held her whilst she cried.

But at the end of each shift, everyone would hang around for a drink, sitting on the sofas in the empty pub. They played their own music and smoked inside, surrounded by chairs stacked on top of tables. April and Noah would chat until sunrise and by the time she got home, she would only sleep for a few hours before having to go back to work again.

'So, you live with your grandparent's?' Noah asked, one evening.

'Yeah, I've lived with them for a couple of years,' April said. Her cheeks flushed, as she took a long swig of her cider. 'I'm not that close with my other folks. I only ever see them at Christmas, or maybe on the odd Sunday.'

'Why's that?' Noah asked.

'Why do you want to know?'

'Because I reckon this is something you've wanted to talk about for a long time,' Noah guessed. 'Just a hunch, though.'

April sighed. 'I've never really told anyone about this. I guess everyone complains about their family, but parent's don't usually forget about their only daughter's birthday, for three years in a row.'

'Jeez. That must've been rough.'

April paused for a moment and then looked straight ahead at Noah. 'It really was,' she admitted. 'I'm at least a decade younger than the rest of my siblings. They spent their whole childhood together, before I eventually came along. So I'm pretty sure I was a disappointment from the moment I was born, because I knew my parents never wanted a fourth child. They were too preoccupied with the others. I did pretty well in school, but it was never enough. I wanted to learn how to bake, but my mum told me that it was a waste of time. No matter how hard I worked, they never gave me the praise that I craved. I always used to think it was my fault, that I wasn't good enough.'

'I'm so sorry to hear that, April.' Noah said. He briefly rested a gentle hand on her shoulder, which she greatly appreciated.

April fished Watson out of her pocket and held him in the palm of her hand. 'My grandpa made this for me. He told me that whenever I hold onto it, I'll be safe and I should remind myself that nothing lasts forever. Not even the bad stuff.'

'I love that. Do you think he could make me one?'

'I think he'd love to!' April put Watson back in her pocket. 'When I moved in with my grandparents, it finally felt like a place I could call home. It's a place of comfort and they were always proud of me. My grandma even taught me how to bake.'

'Those brownies you brought in

tonight were amazing, by the way.' Noah quickly added. 'You should open up your own bakery.'

'I wish!' April laughed. Then, she sighed. 'But I'm so much happier, living with my grandparents. I spent so long at my parent's trying to strive for perfection and they never wanted to know.'

'Perfection doesn't exist!' Jamie announced, as he drunkenly stumbled up from the cellar holding an empty bottle of rum, with two supervisors behind him. 'If we were all perfect, we'd be robots!'

'Oh God, he's gonna get political again, isn't he?' April muttered to Noah, as they watched Jamie crash into the bar. 'Last time, he tried to convince me that the government were slowly turning us into androids.'

'You gotta admit though, Drunk-Jamie is much more entertaining. Normally, he's so monotone.' Noah chuckled. Then, he looked back at April and gave her a comforting smile. 'But he's right. Nothing in life is perfect because we all have our flaws. But that's what makes us human; we're able to show emotion and share our empathy. Our imperfections make us who we are but that doesn't lessen our worth. If you spend your entire life trying to be perfect, you'll miss out on all the joys of life. You'll lose that part of you, that makes you unique.'

'I never realised how knowledgeable you are,' April teased, giving him a friendly nudge.

'I've had a lot of life lessons over the years.'

'Oh, really?'

Noah put his pint to one side and stared down at his lap. He closed his eyes, lowered his head and as a gentle tear rolled down his cheek, April quickly wiped it away. Both of them knew that they were in an understanding and safe place.

'I guess it's my turn to tell you my life story,' Noah said, quietly.

'You don't have to, if you don't

wanna,' April replied, reassuringly. 'We can always change the subject and talk about dragons?'

'Nah, it's okay. But I appreciate it. It's just when I was a teenager, I struggled a lot with anxiety and depression.'

Suddenly, Noah went quiet and absentmindedly began biting his nails. When April gently took his hands away from his mouth, he graciously smiled at her.

'It's ok.' April said, reassuringly. 'I'm listening to whatever you want to tell me.'

'Thanks. I'd never used to speak to anyone about it, because I'd myself to just get over it and be a man. But what does that even mean, anyway? It's so much more than just feeling sad. I lost all motivation to do anything because I was constantly exhausted from overthinking everything. I told myself that I'd never do well, so what was the point in trying anyway? My grades were bad so I dropped out of school. I trapped myself in cages which I'd built myself, convinced that the world was a dangerous place to live in.'

'So what changed?' April asked, gently.

'It was my eighteenth birthday.' Noah replied, with a smile. 'The moment I woke up, I thought: Why am I keeping myself imprisoned and stopping myself from having fun, when there's so much out there to explore? I'd grown up watching documentaries about explorers who showed me all the hidden wonders of the world. I wanted to be just like them, but I told myself I wouldn't be able to do it. But how would I ever know, without even trying? I was the one who was stopping myself from enjoying my life and I'd had enough. So on that night, I destroyed those walls, broke free and decided to explore the world. From then on, it just felt right. I felt like I could be me and ever since then, I've been going wherever life takes me. At first it was terrifying but was exciting. It's not perfect, but nothing ever is. I'm not cured, because I still have good days and bad days. But I'm not afraid to talk about it and I've recently started seeing a therapist. I know that my depression has lied to me, for long enough. Telling me that I wasn't good enough and when I finally challenged that, it was wrong. But I'm happier than I've ever been.'

April and Noah clinked their glasses and finished their drinks. They hugged and it felt warm and safe for both of them because in that moment, they knew that their friendship had bloomed into something wonderful.

'I'm really glad I could tell you all this, Noah.'

'Me too. So what's your favourite dragon?'

'I like Smaug, from *The Hobbit*. He's kinda badass,' April replied. 'What about you?'

Noah thought about this, for a few seconds. 'Puff the Magic Dragon.' he replied, confidently and they both chuckled.

'Look everyone!' Someone screamed.

'April's gonna get it on with the bouncer. You know, if you shag him, it ain't gonna make you better at your job.'

April looked over at Noah and rolled her eyes. God, she despised some of the people she worked with and showed the annoying girl her middle finger.

'Don't you ever take the day off from being a bitch?' she replied. When she looked back at Noah, he was trying to hold back his laughter.

'I never liked her,' April muttered.

'Just ignore them,' Noah replied. 'We got each other. We don't need anyone else.'

*

Over the years, April and Noah's friendship grew stronger and stronger. Everyone at The Two Arrows were convinced that they'd get together but were proved wrong when they became best friends. Sometimes, they would argue or say the wrong thing, but they always made up and moved on. Soon enough, Noah become a part of April's family and her grandparents loved him, too. Being at April's grandparents was the only place that felt like home for the both of them. They would chat for hours and watch thunderstorms, together. There was always a place at the table and a bed set up for Noah when he needed it.

But what truly connected April and Noah was their love of music. On days off, they would spend hours listening to second-hand vinyl's that they scoured at various jumble sales. They went to local rock concerts together and stayed out until the early hours of the morning. They sang classic rock at their local karaoke bar; they danced to Bon Jovi and sang Queen until their voices were sore.

Even through the bad times, April and Noah were always there for each other. Throughout every breakup or after every family gathering, Noah would hold April close whilst she cried; he always knew how she liked her tea and what to say to boost her confidence.

April would meet Noah after intense therapy sessions or stay with him on the bad days; they'd watch countless nature documentaries, grateful to be in each other's company. They always understood each other better than anyone else.

Of course, Noah was the ring-bearer on April's wedding day and was the one who walked her down the aisle. During the ceremony, he sat at the front, next to her grandparents. Standing at the altar, April quickly glanced over her husband's shoulder and grinned at her best friend. Noah wiped a tear from his eye and beamed back at her.

Towards the end of the reception, whilst everyone danced merrily into the night, April dragged Noah away.

'I have to tell you something.' April said, as she sat on a brick wall with her legs dangling.

'It must be important. You dragged me away from *Boogie Wonderland,*' Noah teased, as he sat next to her.

April closed her eyes. She tried to

think of the words to say, but she didn't know how. He was her best friend and she'd never hidden anything from him, before. But this was one of the hardest things, April had ever had to do.

'What is it?' Noah asked.

'Okay. In the next few weeks, I'm going to be opening my new bakery…'

Noah gasped in delight and his eyes widened in ecstasy. 'April, that's incredible! I'm so proud of you.'

'It's in Fawn's Hill,' she quickly added. Just hearing how delighted he was for her, made her heart ache.

'That's quite far away.'

'Yeah, I know, so we're gonna move there. It's also closer to his office, so it seems like the perfect place to settle down.'

Noah didn't say anything, for several moments and looked down at his shoes, lost in his thoughts. A part of April thought that he was going to cry. But then he looked back at her, with a big, heartfelt grin on his face.

'I'm so happy for you, April,' he said,

sincerely.

'A part of me doesn't want to go,' April admitted. She gently rested her head on Noah's bicep.

'Well, what do you want?'

April began to chew her nails and gently, Noah took her hands away from her mouth. She looked up at him with tears in her eyes, which she quickly wiped away. 'I want to go back in time, to when we worked together at The Two Arrows. When it was just me and you, against the world. We thought we were unstoppable.'

'You should've said. I just got rid of my time-machine,' Noah teased. 'Also, you left the pub over three years ago. It wouldn't be the same this time, because life is always gonna move forward, even if you're desperate to go back. This is the start of a brand new chapter in your life. You need to take this. Owning a bakery is something you've always wanted and you've worked so hard for it.'

'I guess.'

'But I'll always be here, cheering you on. Woop-Woop.'

April smiled. 'Thanks. But I don't even want to think about leaving you and everything behind. I've made a home for myself, with you and at my grandparents. I'm scared, Noah.'

'It's gonna be scary. But it's also exciting. You're fearless, April Bloom. And you're gonna carry that with you, wherever you go. Never forget that.'

'What about you?'

'I'll probably just keep doing what I do. See where life takes me and do what feels right for me. Who knows what that'll be?'

'Do you think you'll do that forever?'

'I'll do it until I get bored.'

'I'm gonna miss you so much.' April said, quietly. 'It'll be weird not seeing you, every day.'

'I'm gonna miss you too. But Fawn's Hill is only an hour's drive. We'll still see each other.'

They hopped down from the wall and hugged each other, comforted by each other's presence and screwing their eyes tight so they wouldn't start crying.

'April?'

'Yeah?'

'Don't forget about me?' his voice began to wobble and she felt him gently kiss the top of her head. She clung on tighter and fought back the tears.

'Never.'

*

The last time they spoke was over Skype, whilst Noah was travelling through New Zealand. It was 6am in Fawn's Hill and April was home alone after her husband had to rush to the office for a business emergency.

'So, what's your plan?' April asked, snuggled on the sofa in her dressing gown. There was sleep in her eyes and her hair was scraped into a topknot.

'You know what I'm like, I don't plan anything,' Noah replied, with the sun shining behind him.

'Your photos look amazing, I'm kind of jealous.'

'Auckland's great. But I wish you were here with me, though.'

'I miss you, bro.'

'I miss you too, sis. How's life in the new place?'

'It's nice…' April replied, half-heartedly. She looked around the living room, at all the cardboard boxes that needed to be unpacked. It didn't quite feel like home, just yet. 'It's a really pretty place and everyone seems friendly.'

'So, completely different to the shit we used to deal with?'

'Yep.' April laughed, thinking back. 'I'm actually going to a charity coffee morning in a few hours and properly meet everyone. I hope they like me.'

'Since when did you care about what other people thought of you?'

'I don't,' April replied, defensively. 'I just want to fit in.'

'They're going to love you, how could they not?'

'Thanks, Noah. Speak soon?'

Noah smiled at April. 'Of course. You

know I've always got time for you.'

'Right back at ya.'

When they both end the call, April watched the rain disappear and the sun slowly emerged through the thunderclouds. Without hearing Noah's voice, April never realised how deafening the silence could be.

III

Saturday, 31st August 2019

April waited patiently for Noah by the window. Although her heart was fluttering rapidly beneath her dress, her stomach was in knots. What would be the first thing she'd say to him, after all this time? Would it be too awkward for them to hug? Or maybe she should tidy herself up, re-do her hair and re-apply her makeup. No, that was ridiculous, because Noah never cared about what she looked like. He was used to seeing April in old band t-shirts and baggy jeans, with a mullet she'd once cut herself, for God's sake. Nowadays, April wouldn't dream of going out like that in Fawn's Hill; not since someone had said that her bum looked saggy in leggings.

April thought back to how she used to be, before she moved to Fawn's Hill. From the way she dressed to the things she said, there was a time in her life when she didn't care about what other people thought of her. She knew that not everybody was going to like her and April was a girl to always speak her mind. Life was too short to care about what other people thought of you and she wouldn't try and suck up to people, just to get them to like her.

But that began to change when she moved to Fawn's Hill. The constant look of judgement soon became unbearable and all April cared about what was other people thought of her. It had been a long time since April felt any kind of fearlessness. Over the last few years, she was so focused on being perfect like everyone else in Fawn's Hill, that she never really thought about messaging Noah or giving him a call. Even though it looked like April had everything she could ever ask for, something was missing; she usually tried to ignore the feeling because she didn't know what it really was. Until tonight.

A wave of guilt ran throughout April's body, at the thought of drifting apart from Noah for so long. Squeezing Watson for reassurance, she continued to watch the thunderstorm. She was so excited to see Noah, but would it be the same, or was it going to be incredibly awkward between them? What if they weren't as close as they used to be?

Noah arrived within the hour. The moment he pulled his car into the driveway, April jumped from the window-sill and flung open the door; for a brief moment all she could do was stare at him. Since the last time she saw him, Noah had lost all his piercings and his hair longer and wilder. He was already drenched from the rain, but his smile still gleamed like a light through the fog. Neither of them said anything, but when he opened out his arms, April knew that this was the same Noah Wisdom she knew and loved. She sprinted out into the rain and ran into his arms. His hugs were still the same, warm and protective. The rain pounded heavily on both of them and even though there were tears in her eyes, April couldn't stop smiling. In that moment, she knew that everything was going to be okay.

'Hey, sis.' Noah chuckled, as he gently lifted April off her feet.

'I've missed you, bro.' April mumbled, her cheeks flushing red.

'Missed you, too. But shall we get out of the rain? I can carry you, if you'd like?'

'Yes please. You're the best.'

With her arms still wrapped around his neck, Noah hauled them both inside and when they broke apart, they dried themselves off. When Noah stepped into the living room, the first thing he did was stare at all the beautifully framed photos on the mantlepiece: April and her husband on their wedding day;

April with her grandparents and photos with the in-laws. But there's one of April and Noah, tucked away at the back; they're sat on the old sofa at April's grandparents, looking hungover from the night before but still happy.

'Oh God, Noah. I've left the place in a right state.' April said, as she stumbled into the living and quickly cleared away the single wine glass on the coffee table. Then she began to tidy away everything that was already in its place, all while blushing profusely. 'I feel like such an idiot.'

'Hey, April.' Noah said, gently. Although she doesn't listen to him, until he put his hands on her shoulders. April looked up at her best friend and when he smiled back at her, it put her mind at rest. 'You don't need to clean up, everything is amazing.'

'But not perfect?'

'It doesn't need to be.'

April opened her mouth to speak, but then her stomach began to rumble.

Noah chuckled. 'You hungry?'

April thought about the artisanal pizzas on the kitchen counter. They were designed on hand-stretched sourdough with beautifully torn mozzarella and accompanied by sundried tomatoes, hand-picked by Italian hunks. They were fancy and expensive, much like everything else in Fawn's Hill. As pretty and artistic as her food looked, April craved a greasy, margherita pizza from her old takeaway. Just thinking of it made her stomach rumble and if she couldn't have a date-night with her husband, at least she could have dinner with Noah. In a flash, she ran to the kitchen to grab them, along with two ciders from the fridge. When she joined Noah on the sofa, her cottage was slowly starting to feel like home.

'It's just like old times.' Noah chuckled, as the two of them helped themselves. 'Cheers, April.'

'No problem. I'm just glad you're here,' April replied, as she scoffed a slice of pizza and swigged her cider. 'I just didn't want to spend another night home alone. It gets a bit lonely sometimes.'

'What about your other friends, in Fawn's Hill?'

'Err… I haven't really got any.'

'You what? I find that hard to believe.'

April opened her mouth to speak but then immediately closed it. She could barely admit it to herself that she wasn't happy. How could she admit it to anyone else? But Noah wasn't just anybody else.

'You know that you can tell me anything, April,' Noah said, reassuringly. 'Don't hold back.'

April slowly leant back on the sofa. She looked up at the ceiling, thought about what to say and then looked back at Noah. 'The thing is, no one really likes me, in Fawn's Hill. I've tried being nice, being myself or being like everyone else. But they don't wanna know about me. I see the way they look at me with their noses in the air. The way they sneer when they say my name and the false smiles behind gritted teeth. But I don't know what to do about it. It's never felt like I belonged here, no matter how hard I tried. Nothing I ever do is good enough so it feels like it's all my fault.'

'April, I can't even think of what you could've done, to make them feel this way?'

'I never told you about what happened at the first Christmas party I went to.'

'What happened?'

April blushed. Even though it happened almost three years ago, it was still her most embarrassing moment and some of the villagers still looked down on her, because of it. It was the reason why April made every effort to get people in Fawn's Hill to like her.

As an attempt to fit in, April went along to the annual Christmas party that was held at the local village hall. She ended up going alone, because her husband was called away on a last-minute business trip. Nevertheless, April still made an attempt to get to know everyone. At first, everything seemed fine, with some awkward small talk and constant forgetting of names. But April had no idea what anyone was talking about and no-one made any effort to include her in the conversation so she found herself at the buffet table, snacking on sausage-rolls. Next to her, was a miserable, old man dressed as Santa who was hired to entertain the children; apparently he hated Christmas and only took the job because he needed the money. They began chatting, got drunk on mulled-wine and before she knew it, they were standing on top of the buffet table, loudly singing Irish Christmas songs. Everyone stared at them, as if they'd gone mad. Someone even ordered her to get down and behave herself. But to make matters worse, April tripped over her heels and face-planted into the trifle. Ultimately, Santa was never allowed back into Fawn's Hill and April spent the rest of the weekend, hibernating in shame under her duvet. Ever since then, not daring to do or say whatever she wanted, she decided to blend in with everyone else.

'You got Santa drunk?' Noah cried, with laughter.

April tried to hide her giggles with a glare and threw a cushion at him. 'It's not funny! They've never forgiven me and it was three bloody years ago!'

'Well, if you can't laugh about it with your friends, then who else can you laugh about it with?'

'I guess…'

'The thing is, that's not even that bad!' Noah cried. 'I've definitely seen you do worse.'

'Thanks, pal,' April replied, sarcastically. 'That party was so boring, anyway. But I do something stupid and they treat me like scum. It's shit.'

'Have you told your fella that you're not happy?' Noah asked, tentatively.

'Haven't had the chance,' April muttered.

'Over the last three years?'

'He practically lives at the office, especially these days. He may as well take his own sleeping bag and kip under his desk.'

'When was the last time you spent time together, just the two of you?'

'Dunno.'

'Well, if you're not happy, then you need to talk to him about this. Take control of the situation.'

'Nothing will change. He's too focused on his job.'

'How do you know? You won't know until you try.'

'Since when did you get so good at relationship advice?' April teased.

A small smile crept across Noah's face, as he looked down and twiddled his thumbs.

April tried to catch his gaze. 'Is there something you're not telling me, Noah?'

'Maybe…' Noah giggled nervously. It was unlike anything April had ever seen before. 'I may have actually met someone…'

'Wait, what?!' April cried. 'Why has it taken this long for you to tell me?'

'We've been together for about six months, but it feels right. I'm one smitten-kitten,' Noah admitted. 'I can't wait for you to finally meet her. I've told her all about you.'

'I want to meet her! How did this happen? You never used to show an interest in anyone?'

'She came along at just the right time,' Noah admitted. 'About a year after you'd left, life began to get lonely. Every job I went to, left me unfulfilled. There wasn't anyone I wanted to make memories with, so I began to isolate myself from the world, again. I was stuck, not knowing what I was going to do next with my life. I was scared that my life was going to turn into Groundhog Day, if I didn't do something about it. But then I met her at a karaoke bar. We sang *Islands in the Stream* and it's been history ever since. She made me see the exciting side of life again and I love her so much for it. So we've decided to The Two Arrows as joint managers.'

'You're gonna manage the pub?' April gasped, her eyes twinkling with excitement.

'I knew I'd go back to that place because it always felt like home. Working there made me feel like I was part of a family. I never wanted to settle down, because I was scared that I'd ruin everything and fall back into that dark place I'd been avoiding for so long. Even now, I still have good days and bad days. But I trust myself and I'm confident to follow my heart. Even though it terrifies me, it's so worth it. And now I've seen you, I'm even happier. I've got some good people in my life and everything's gonna be okay.'

'I'm so happy for you Noah.' April said, before her heart began to fill with sadness. She slowly dropped her chin to her chest, her eyes filling with tears.

'What's the matter?' Noah asked.

'I'm sorry.'

'What are you sorry for?'

'For not speaking to you for so long. We used to be inseparable, but I was so focused on wanting to be liked in Fawn's Hill that I didn't even send you a text. It's all my fault…'

'Hey,' Noah replied, softly. 'I'm gonna stop you there, before you start spiralling into misery. I'm not mad at you, April. You were busy living your life and I was with mine. So, does that mean you're mad at me?'

'No, of course not.'

'Just because our lives went in different directions, doesn't mean to say our friendship had to end. Our friendship was never lost, April. We were always going to be there for each other. You've always been my best friend.'

'And you've always been mine,' April admitted. 'I was so nervous about seeing you, tonight. But it feels just like it used to. I was worried things would've changed and it wouldn't be the same.'

'People are gonna change throughout the years, but that's just life. We might change the way we dress and think a little differently. We all move onto new chapters in our lives. But there's a core part of us that stays the same, no matter what. We carry it around with us, always. I can still see yours, April. You're still as fearless as ever.'

'I haven't felt that way, in years,' April admitted. 'I just wanted to be perfect, like everyone else.'

'You may not feel it, but I know it's still there. In ways that you didn't expect,' Noah reassured her. 'You've picked yourself up, when you were knocked down. You successfully run your own business, put yourself out there and worked so hard for it. You're still just as fearless, April Bloom.' Noah slowly leant back on the sofa and kept his eyes on her. 'Do you remember what Jamie once said?'

'Jamie spoke a lot of crap.'

'True. But he said that perfection doesn't exist and even though we don't want to admit it, he's right. No one in this world is perfect. There isn't one perfect way to live your life and we've all done stupid stuff at one point. But this idea of perfection is just a façade, an expectation that we'll never reach. It stunts you from being the best person that you can be because you're too busy trying to convince everyone else that you have it all. But by accepting that not everything can be perfect, we can appreciate the good things we have in our lives.'

April gave Noah a small smile. 'I'm really glad you're here, tonight. There's so much I've needed to say and I just hadn't found the right person to say it.'

'I'm glad you can tell me. It's like we were never apart.'

'Whatever happened to Jamie, do you know? April asked.

'Last time I heard he was working on an alpaca farm.'

'Bloody hell. So I guess he doesn't scream about the death of capitalism anymore?'

'When I went to go and visit him, he told me that he'd finally found his zen. He even named an alpaca after me.'

'I guess we're all growing up. It had to happen someday.'

'But that doesn't mean we still can't have fun.' Noah reassured her.

'Cheers to that.' April and Noah clinked their glasses and downed them, quickly.

'I see you've still got your old vinyl player.' Noah slowly wandered over to it on the other side of the room. 'I remember when you bought it for twenty quid at the jumble sale.'

'I'll never get rid of it,' April replied. 'But I haven't played anything on there in ages.'

'Can I?'

'Sure.'

Noah flicked through the row of vinyl's but the moment he decided to put on The Killers, April let out a shriek of excitement and jumped over to him.

'I haven't listened to this in years!' she cried and began to dance to the first song.

'Seriously?' Noah asked, as he twirled April around. 'We were obsessed with them back in the day!'

April turned the volume on *Mr. Brightside* and the two of them sang every word at the top of their voices. They jumped around like fools and either flailed their arms, swung each other around until they were dizzy or serenaded each other on the stairs. They even stood on the kitchen table and remembered the routine they once made up, when they used to go clubbing. Just from dancing into the night, gave April a sense of freedom from her worries.

When the two of them were completely out of breath, they sat by the windowsill and watched the thunderstorm. The lightning wasn't as prominent, but the rain was still heavy and the sound of the thunder was comforting.

'Do you still have Watson?' Noah asked.

April dug the crochet octopus out of

her pocket. She held him in her lap and smiled. 'Of course. I don't go anywhere without him.'

'Unless you lose him?' Noah joked.

'That was one time, you bastard.'

'Just think, if I hadn't found him, we may have never been friends.'

April looked out at the thunderstorm and smiled back at Noah. She could feel a warm sensation trickle over her entire body, as if someone had put a warm blanket over her. All this time, Noah was the fulfilment she always needed. The friend that knew April the best.

'Nah, we were destined to meet at some point. I can't see my life without you in it,' April eventually replied. 'But what about you? Have you still got yours?'

Noah reached into his shirt pocket and showed April the emerald green, crochet octopus in the palm of his hand. April noticed that Noah's octopus looked a lot more worn from the years gone by, but still well-loved.

'I take this little guy everywhere I go,'

he said. 'It reminds me of when we would hang out at your grandparent's.'

'They loved you…' April said. Her voice trailed off as she gazed deeply into the thunderstorm. Since moving to Fawn's Hill, she only ever saw her grandparent's once a year. Every time she tried to visit them more often, something always cropped up: her husband had planned a last-minute dinner party with Martin or there was a village charity event that she had to attend. It seemed that April had given up a lot to move to Fawn's Hill. 'I miss them so much.'

'Then why don't we find a day and go visit them?' Noah kindly suggested. 'We can play monopoly and even watch the thunderstorm if there is one.'

'Sounds good, but maybe not monopoly?' April giggled. 'I remember the last time we played it almost broke their marriage!'

'Well, I promise you'll see them soon.'

Unlike her husband, April believed Noah's promises, this time. They may not have seen each other in so long but they always made time for each other.

'And I promise that we'll see each other, more often,' April added.

'Sounds good, sis.'

April looked out at the thunderstorm and sighed. 'It's a shame we can't go out tonight. I could've shown you around.'

'What's stopping us?'

'Have you looked outside?'

'I trekked through the rain to get to you.'

'That's true, but you drove here. We can't go wandering out into the rain.'

'That's never stopped us before.'

'It's late. The neighbours will see us.'

'So what? Who cares about what people will think of us?'

April looked at Noah and a cheeky grin began to grow on her face. Tonight, she was able to escape all the pressure she'd put herself under and she could finally spread her wings and fly free. All she ever needed was to have fun with her best friend and forget about everything else. Besides, who were they offending?

'Let's do it.' April replied, firmly.

Quickly, she stuffed her feet into her wellies, grabbed Noah by the hand and they ran outside. The rain was freezing cold and the wind was swift, but that didn't stop them from jumping into the first puddle that they could find. It wasn't long before April and Noah became completely drenched, but they were also crying with laughter. In a drunken flurry, they ran through the streets of Fawn's Hill and slurred the words to *Purple Rain*. Noah swung April onto his back and as she clung onto her legs, she sat up straight and threw her arms in the air. Even though she was shivering, April sang even louder to warm herself up. Her mascara was running down her cheeks and her hair was plastered to her face.

'Woo-Hoo!' she cried. 'Best. Night. Ever!'

'April Bloom. What on earth are you doing at this time of night?'

Noah spun them both around and

April could see one of the villagers standing in her doorway. Was that the woman who complained that April had put indigo blue icing on her son's Christening cake, instead of denim blue? April could sense the piercing glare, coming from the old crone. She knew that it would probably turn into hot gossip by morning. But April didn't care.

'Oh, shut up. I'm having fun!' She cried and threw her middle finger up to the sky.

'You will never live this down, April Bloom!' another villager cried, from his window. He was the one who wouldn't invite April to his birthday party because she didn't know the complete history of Fawn's Hill.

'Shove it up your arse!' April cried, with laughter. She slipped off Noah's back and they sprinted back to the house. Jumping in every puddle along the way and laughing like they used to.

'It seems like you've wanted to say

that for a long time?' Noah asked.

'I really have.'

IV

Sunday, 1ˢᵗ September, 2019

Snuggled on the sofa in her dressing gown, April woke up with a smile on her face. She was still wearing the same clothes from last night. Her back ached from sleeping in an awkward position and she could only feel her legs once she slowly stretched them out. It was all accompanied by the worst headache, but April was too happy to care.

The last thing she remembered was stumbling into the living room, hanging onto Noah's arm and laughing so hard that they could barely breathe.

She looked over at Noah, who had nestled himself in the armchair under a small mountain of blankets. She was extremely grateful for him, not just from last night but from the moment they met at The Two Arrows and everything they had been through together since then.

Noah was the piece of happiness that was missing from April's life and she wasn't going to let him go again.

She went to the kitchen and poured two glasses of water with lots of ice, leaving one at Noah's side as he slept peacefully. Then, April sat in her garden and looked up at the morning sun shining through the wispy clouds, whilst breathing in the scent of dew on the grass. Last night's thunderstorm meant that April's wildflowers could bloom beautifully.

As she slowly sipped her water, April felt the nourishment coursing through her body and mind. The butterflies in her stomach were floating away, releasing all the nervousness that was trapped within her. Her head felt lighter because she was able to speak her mind. For a few blissful moments, April just enjoyed the peace and quiet.

'Morning,' Noah said, as he eventually joined April and sat next to her.

'Morning, bro. How did you sleep?'

'My legs feel like jelly, but I don't know if that's from all the dancing or sleeping in an armchair.' Noah chuckled. 'What about you?'

'A bit hungover but it was so worth it,' April admitted. 'I think last night was destined to happen.'

'Me too. It was everything I needed.'

Flashes from last night began to play in April's mind. 'Did we dance to The Killers?' she asked.

'Yep. You also told me the story of the Christmas party and we went jumping in puddles.'

'Oh, God. I haven't done anything like that in a long time. Fawn' Hill will never forgive me.' April laughed, the smile still shining on her face. For some reason, she didn't feel ashamed or embarrassed. Spending last night with Noah made her feel free. 'Fancy going for a walk and grabbing a hot-chocolate?' she asked.

'Sure.'

In the space of ten minutes, April brushed her teeth, scraped her hair into a bun and pulled on her tracksuit bottoms. It felt nice not to worry about what she looked like, for once.

They linked arms and walked through Fawn's Hill, with the blinding sun soaking up all the puddles scattered across the cobbled floor. April could see her nosy neighbours peeking from behind their curtains, all with a scathing expression. When they got to the café, a group of Yoga-Mums gathered around a table, simultaneously rolled their eyes at the sight of them.

'They don't like me because when I went to one of their classes, I fell asleep in child's pose,' April muttered to Noah, as they patiently waited in the queue. The two of them giggled like schoolchildren.

'Good morning,' Noah said, as they cheerfully approached the barista behind the counter. 'Two hot chocolates to go, please.'

'Everyone could hear the racket you were making last night, April,' the barista mentioned, completely ignoring

Noah, as she steamed the milk and cocoa powder.

'It was fun, though,' April admitted, without shame. 'You should've joined us.'

'Well, some of us just don't have the time to be so frivolous.' The barista slammed two hot-chocolates down in front of them, followed by a patronising smile. 'But it must be so nice not to care about what other people think of you. Cash or card?'

April's cheeks flushed scarlet as she quickly paid and tried to scuttle away.

'Jeez. Let's get out of here.' Noah muttered, just loud enough for April to hear.

'Oh, April?' one of the Yoga-Mum's called out, without even looking in her direction. 'Do let us know when you're expecting to grow up and not waste your time acting so ridiculously with other men. We really don't want you bringing down the standard of this town any further. You look a right state.'

'I was having fun!' April suddenly blurted out to the entire café and everyone stared at her, as if she'd gone mad. But even though with trembling knees and a pounding heart, April just couldn't bare to keep it all to herself, anymore. She was sick and tired of being judged by everyone, for everything she'd said and done. It finally felt good to tell them exactly what was on her mind. 'Bloody hell, you should try it, sometime!'

April stormed out of the café, with a wicked smile on her face. Whilst Noah awkwardly stood by the door, shuffling from one foot to the other and clutching onto his hot chocolate.

'Err, it was lovely to meet you all,' Noah mumbled, as he scuttled out and swiftly caught up with April. 'Was that worth it?' He asked her.

'Yep. I'm worth more than that,' April replied, confidently.

'Good girlie. But I have a funny feeling that they might think I'm your secret lover, or something.'

'What? Because a guy and a girl spent time together, just the two of them? Let them believe what they want to believe. You and I know the truth.'

'Yeah, you're right. Plus, you always need to find the time to be frivolous,' Noah said, mocking the barista. The two of them laughed. 'So where are we heading?'

'I know a place.'

April led Noah up the hill and when they got to the top, they sat on a bench that overlooked the entire village. They slowly drank their hot chocolates in peaceful silence, both grateful for the other's company. April had so much fun last night, and she didn't need to post about it on Instagram to prove it. In her heart, she would always cherish the night she felt fearless, once again.

'What's on your mind?' Noah asked.

April looked up at her oldest and dearest friend. She smiled and gently rested her head on his bicep. 'Last night meant everything to me because it was the first time since moving here that I was able to let go. You were the one who allowed me to do that. I'm so grateful for you and I always have been.'

'Last night meant a lot for me too. But give yourself credit, April. You were the one who called me, after all. Maybe it was because you'd had enough of trying to please everyone all the time.'

'They say that nothing lasts forever. But I reckon our friendship will last a lifetime. We'll make sure of that.'

April happily swung her legs and gripped onto the bench until it dug into her palms, double-checking that this moment was real. She looked out at the rolling hills and the life that lies beyond Fawn's Hill. They could go anywhere together and feel unstoppable. April thought back to their late night shopping at Tesco's, where they'd ride their trolley down every aisle. Or when they suffered through stressful shifts at The Two Arrows together, they'd still find a reason to laugh. Such mundane moments turned into unforgettable memories. April looked back at Noah and her heart and soul were filled with joy. She could never let him go, no matter how far apart they were.

'I've missed you, bro.' April mumbled.

'I've missed you, too. But we'll never drift again.'

'Never.'

*

Eventually, April and Noah slowly walked backed home, arms linked and smiling. They chatted the entire way, ignoring the judgemental looks from all the other villagers. Even though they knew it wasn't the end, they still savoured every moment spent together before going their separate ways. Just before Noah got into his car, they shared one last hug and stayed there for as long as possible. The warmth the two of them shared was comforting and neither of them wanted to let go. April had her arms wrapped around his chest, whilst Noah gently kissed the top of her head and nestled his nose in her hair.

'Let's not say goodbye,' Noah said. 'because I know I'll see you soon.'

'Hopefully before the next thunderstorm,' April teased.

'I can't wait. Cheerio, April.'

'Toodle-oo, Noah.'

Eventually, April stood in her doorway and watched Noah drive off. Then, she slowly wandered into her house, slumped onto the sofa and held onto the warm, fuzzy feeling that was slowly taking over her entire body. Even though she was alone, she wasn't lonely because there was a fulfilment growing in her heart.

She quickly checked her phone and saw a string of messages from her husband stating that Martin was a prick, and April couldn't help but agree. In fact, it wasn't long until her husband came back and the minute he saw her, a smile lit up on his face. He quickly wrapped his arms around April and kissed her passionately. It took her by surprise but she happily kissed him back.

'What brought all that on?' April asked, as they broke apart but still remained close.

'I really missed you, last night,' her husband admitted. He snuggled into her arms and April held him close. 'Work was so stressful but being back with you was what got me through it.'

April gently stroked her husband's hair, trying to think of what to say to him. If she didn't say anything now, when would she?

'Babe? There's something I need to talk to you about,' April said, softly.

'What is it?'

April took a deep breath and told him everything. How she felt about living in Fawn's Hill and never feeling like she could fit in because she wasn't good enough. Even though it felt like she had it all, April knew in herself, that she wasn't truly happy. She also spoke about how lonely she was when her husband constantly went back to the office. Although her heart was racing and her hands were trembling, the words came pouring out of her mouth and April felt a sense of relief, not to hold back. If she didn't tell him, how was he supposed to know how she was feeling? Her husband listened intently to every word she said, holding her close and interlacing his fingers with hers. When she was done, he looked deeply into her eyes.

'Baby, why didn't you tell me any of this before?' he asked.

'I didn't want to be a bother. Besides, I know how much your work means to you.'

'I care about where I work, but no more than I care about you.'

'I just wanted to spend more time with you. You're all I've got, living here.'

'So how about I promise to not let work get in the way, so we can spend more time together? I know we've not properly seen each other recently and I've missed you.'

April kissed her husband on the

cheek. She could feel her heart getting lighter already. 'Sounds good, babe. But I also want to find more time to go and see my grandparents. I've only seen them once, this year.'

'We'll drive down to see them, or they can spend the weekend here. I promise you, this time.'

'I love you.'

'I love you, too. But now you have to promise me not to stress yourself out about trying to fit in with everyone else. I've noticed how much pressure you put on yourself, but you don't need to prove yourself to anyone. You're wonderful and always good enough for me.'

April blushed. 'I'll work on it. So we're gonna have a date night sooner rather than later?'

'If work calls me again after hours, I'll tell them no. Martin needs to start doing shit.'

'You know he's a twat, right?'

'Well, we won't be having him or his missus over for dinner any time soon.'

The two of them laugh and kissed

again, lingering for as long as possible. April couldn't remember the last time she felt this intimate with him.

'So how was your night?' her husband asked. 'You look exhausted.'

April's phone gently buzzed and saw it was a text from Noah, asking if she was free to do karaoke next weekend. She smiled to herself and looked at the vinyl player, the empty plates and bottles on the table and then at the windowsill. She took Watson out of her pocket and gently rolled him between her fingers. Then, she looked back at her husband.

'It was everything I needed.'

The End.

Acknowledgements

I am so proud to share *The Octopus and the Thunderstorm* with you all and I have so many people to thank:

First of all, I want to thank my family for always being so supportive and giving me a push in the right direction. They have always known my love for writing and I would never have finished my book if it wasn't for their encouragement.

I also want to thank my friends, who have always stuck by me, through it all. My love for writing about friendship is definitely inspired by them and I'm so very grateful for it. As well as a massive thank you to my partner, Zach, who has been my rock through all of this.

A thank you to anyone who has ever asked me about how my writing is going. It really means a lot to me, when I hear that people are interested in what I do.

Thank you to Joey Howard for creating such an amazing book cover! I love what you have created and it was such a pleasure to work with you, on this creative project.

Also, a thank you to my editor, Deborah Blake. You are incredible to work with and for providing an excellent editing service, as always.

Finally, dear reader. Thank you, for taking the time to read *The Octopus and the Thunderstorm*. I hope you enjoyed reading this book as much as I enjoyed writing it.

Love Carrie.

About the Author

Growing up, Carrie was always coming up with stories and her love for books has never changed. She graduated from UWTSD Lampeter in 2018, with a BA in Classical Studies, focusing on Greek mythology and ancient Greek literature. During her final year, she loved to write stories and in April 2021, she self-published her first book *The Author's Library*.

Nowadays, you can usually find her snuggled up with a good book and a cup of tea. She's also been blogging since 2015 about books, musings of life and anything that she finds curious. Carrie also loves to travel the world when she can and is always seeking the next adventure.

Carrie Duggan currently lives in London.

Printed in Great Britain
by Amazon